Dex
and the
Funfair

Written by Paul Shipton
Illustrated by Richard Watson

Dex, Meg and Jaz go to the funfair.

Bump!

They go on the bumper cars.
Then they go on the helter-skelter.

WIN A PURE
DEAR DOLL

Then Jaz sees the best thing.
"Look! I will win a Pure Dear doll,"
she tells Dex and Meg.

They all go to the cans.
Jaz aims at the tin cans but ...

Dex looks at the cans. "This is unfair," he thinks. "The cans are stuck down with gum!"

Dex has a go next.

SMASH! Dex hits a cup.

CRASH! He hits a dish.

Then Dex hits the fair man.
"Ow! My rear!"

"Stop!" the man tells Dex. "You will smash all my gear. Just go!"

And the fair man hands a
Pure Dear doll to Dex.

Dex, Jaz and Meg go.
"How did you miss, Dex? You are
the best shot."

"I did not miss," Dex tells Jaz.
"I was not aiming at the cans!"